SPORTS ZONE
SPECIAL REPORT

BBL
BASKETBALL

PNT
PAINTBALL

SKT
SKATEBOARDING

BSL
BASEBALL

HKY
HOCKEY

FULLER'S FORMER TEAM AIMS TO EMBARRASS HIM ON COURT

ZACK FULLER

STATS:
TEAM: TIGERS
AGE: 13
NUMBER: 44
POSITION: SMALL FORWARD

BIO: Zack is a defensive specialist. He averages 3.5 blocked shots and 2.75 steals per game, and always guards the opposition's best players. But Zack's former team, the Bulldogs, are coming to town, and they think Zack's a traitor for joining the Tigers. To make matters worse, Zack will have to guard his former best friend, Joey Jacobs, who is an ultra-quick sharpshooter.

UP NEXT: *FULL COURT PRESSURE*

JOEY
JACOBS

TEAM: BULLDOGS
AGE: 14
NUMBER: 13
POSITION: POINT GUARD
ROLE: TEAM CAPTAIN

BLZ vs BKS
3-1
TGR vs RDR
33-32
EAG vs BAN
14-7
SPA vs WLD
4-3
BAN vs RDR
21-15
RDR vs LIG
4-3
BLZ vs BKS
3-1

BIO: Joey Jacobs may be the most difficult player in the league to guard. He loves to draw fouls with his lightning-quick head-fakes so he can get to the free-throw line, where he hits nearly 90 percent of his shots. Joey will be out for revenge against his former friend, Zack, when his Bulldogs battle the Tigers.

PERRY BOYD

TEAM: TIGERS **AGE:** 14 **NO:** 77 **POSITION:** SHOOTING GUARD
BIO: Perry Boyd is the Tigers' team captain and top playmaker. When this streaky shooter starts sinking shots, the points begin to pile up.

BOYD

ALFONSO HECTOR

TEAM: TIGERS **AGE:** 46 **POSITION:** COACH
BIO: Alfonso Hector is a no-nonsense coach who has a knack for bringing out the best in his players.

COACH

PRESENTS

FULL COURT
PRESSURE

A PRODUCTION OF

STONE ARCH BOOKS
a capstone imprint

written by *Jessica Gunderson*
illustrated by *Alfonso Ruiz*
colored by *Jorge Gonzalez*

designed and directed by *Bob Lentz*
edited by *Sean Tulien*
creative direction by *Heather Kindseth*
editorial direction by *Michael Dahl*

Sports Illustrated Kids *Full Court Pressure* is published by Stone Arch Books,
151 Good Counsel Drive, P.O. Box 669, Mankato, Minnesota 56002.
www.capstonepub.com

Summary: Star defensive player Zack Fuller is in a tough spot. His new
Tigers teammates don't trust him. The players on the Bulldogs, his old
squad, think he's a traitor for leaving. When the two teams face each other
in the playoffs, Zack has to guard his former best friend. To make matters
worse, the Tigers captain refuses to pass the ball to Zack. Caught between
a Tiger and a Bulldog, and in serious foul trouble, Zack will have to find a
way to play through the pressure.

Cataloging-in-Publication Data is available on the Library of Congress
website.

ISBN: 978-1-4342-1911-4 (library binding)
ISBN: 978-1-4342-2291-6 (paperback)

Printed in the United States of America in Stevens Point, Wisconsin.
092009   005619WZS10

SHARP-SHOOTING TIGERS AND THE ULTRA-AGGRESSIVE BULLDOGS   SIK *TICKER*

11

16

At halftime...

We're only down by two! This is our game to win.

Perry's on fire today.

When we're on offense, Perry needs to touch the ball on every possession.

At the beginning of the third quarter...

. . . and Perry Boyd scores!

Suddenly . . .

AAHHH!

WHEEET!!

Perry!

SPORTS ZONE

POSTGAME RECAP

BBL
BASKETBALL

PNT
PAINTBALL

SKT
SKATEBOARDING

BSL
BASEBALL

HKY
HOCKEY

FULLER

FULLER OVERCOMES FOUL TROUBLE TO WIN STATE TITLE FOR TIGERS!

BY THE NUMBERS

FINAL SCORE:
TIGERS: 74
BULLDOGS: 73

GAME HIGHS:
POINTS: BOYD, 22
FOULS: FULLER, 4
BLOCKS: FULLER, 5

STORY:

Zack Fuller survived early foul trouble to score the game-winning free throws after time had expired. The win gives the Tigers their first ever state title. Team captain, Perry Boyd, was quoted as saying, "Zack really stepped up his game today. We couldn't have won without him."

UP NEXT: SI KIDS INFO CENTER

SZ POSTGAME EXTRA
WHERE **YOU** ANALYZE THE GAME!

BLZ vs BRS
3-1
TGR vs ROR
33-32
EAG vs BAN
14-7
SPA vs WLD
4-3
BAN vs ROR
21-15
RZR vs LIG
4-3
BLZ vs BRS

Basketball fans witnessed an exciting game today when Zack clinched the win for the Tigers from the free-throw line. Let's go into the stands and ask some fans for their thoughts on the day's events...

DISCUSSION QUESTION 1
Zack has to compete against his best friend, Joey Jacobs. Have you ever competed against a friend? Can opponents also be friends with each other?

DISCUSSION QUESTION 2
Zack had to transfer to a new school after his family moved. Was it fair for Joey Jacobs to be angry at Zack for switching schools? Why or why not?

WRITING PROMPT 1
Perry Boyd injures his ankle during the big game. Have you ever gotten injured? What were you doing when it happened? Write about it.

WRITING PROMPT 2
Zack wins the big game for the Tigers. Have you ever won a contest or competition? What did you do? How did it make you feel? Write about your experience.

GLOSSARY

ASSET (ASS-et)—something or someone who is helpful or useful

CHARGING (CHAHR-jing)—a foul which occurs when an offensive player runs into a defender who has established position

FORMER (FOR-mur)—previous or earlier

HEAD-FAKE (HED-FAYK)—a faked shot attempt used to trick a defending player into thinking a shot is coming

RUIN (ROO-in)—to spoil or destroy something completely

THREAT (THRET)—a warning that punishment or harm will follow if a certain thing is done or not done

TRAITOR (TRAY-tur)—someone who betrays a friend, team, or trust

CREATORS

JESSICA GUNDERSON › Author

Jessica Gunderson grew up in North Dakota. She is currently a writer and teacher in Madison, Wisconsin, where she lives with her husband and her cat.

ALFONSO RUIZ › Illustrator

Alfonso Ruiz was born in Macuspana, Tabasco in Mexico, where the temperature is just as hot as the sauce is. He became a comic book illustrator when he was 17 years old, and has worked on many graphic novels since then. Alfonso has illustrated several English graphic novels, including retellings of Dracula and Pinocchio.

JORGE GONZALEZ › Colorist

Jorge Gonzalez was born in Monterrey, Mexico. Jorge began his career as a colorist for the graphic novel retellings of *The Time Machine* and *Journey to the Center of the Earth*. In 2006, Jorge, along with several other artists, established Protobunker Studio, where he currently works as a colorist.